The
United Nations

Global Leadership

UN Action Against Terrorism
Fighting Fear

by Heather Docalavich

Mason Crest Publishers
Philadelphia

Mason Crest Publishers Inc.
370 Reed Road
Broomall, Pennsylvania 19008
(866) MCP-BOOK (toll free)
www.masoncrest.com

13 12 11 10 09 08 07   10 9 8 7 6 5 4 3 2

Library of Congress Cataloging-in-Publication Data

Docalavich, Heather.
  UN action against terrorism : fighting fear / by Heather Docalavich.
    p. cm. — (The United Nations—global leadership)
  Includes index.
        ISBN 978-1-4222-0067-4
        ISBN 978-1-4222-0065-0 (series)
  1. Terrorism—Prevention—International cooperation—Juvenile literature. 2. United Nations—Juvenile literature. 3. War on Terrorism, 2001—Juvenile literature. 4. Security, International—Juvenile literature. 5. Humanitarian assistance—Juvenile literature. I. Title. II. Series.
  HV6431.D84 2007
  363.32—dc22
                                2005029012

Interior design by Benjamin Stewart.
Interiors produced by Harding House Publishing Service, Inc.
www.hardinghousepages.com
Cover design by Peter Culatta.
Printed in the Hashemite Kingdom of Jordan.

Contents

Introduction
by Dr. Bruce Russett

The United Nations was founded in 1945 by the victors of World War II. They hoped the new organization could learn from the mistakes of the League of Nations that followed World War I—and prevent another war.

The United Nations has not been able to bring worldwide peace; that would be an unrealistic hope. But it has contributed in important ways to the world's experience of more than sixty years without a new world war. Despite its flaws, the United Nations has contributed to peace.

Like any big organization, the United Nations is composed of many separate units with different jobs. These units make three different kinds of contributions. The most obvious to students in North America and other democracies are those that can have a direct and immediate impact for peace.

Especially prominent is the Security Council, which is the only UN unit that can authorize the use of military force against countries and can require all UN members to cooperate in isolating an aggressor country's economy. In the Security Council, each of the big powers—Britain, China, France, Russia, and the United States—can veto any proposed action. That's because the founders of United Nations recognized that if the Council tried to take any military action against the strong opposition of a big power it would result in war. As a result, the United Nations was often sidelined during the Cold War era. Since the end of the Cold War in 1990, however, the Council has authorized many military actions, some directed against specific aggressors but most intended as more neutral peacekeeping efforts. Most of its peacekeeping efforts have been to end civil wars rather than wars between countries. Not all have succeeded, but many have. The United Nations Secretary-General also has had an important role in mediating some conflicts.

UN units that promote trade and economic development make a different kind of contribution. Some help to establish free markets for greater prosperity, or like the UN Development Programme, provide economic and technical assistance to reduce poverty in poor countries. Some are especially concerned with environmental problems or health issues. For example, the World Health Organization and UNICEF deserve great credit for eliminating the deadly disease of smallpox from the world. Poor countries especially support the United Nations for this reason. Since many wars, within and between countries, stem from economic deprivation, these efforts make an important indirect contribution to peace.

Still other units make a third contribution: they promote human rights. The High Commission for Refugees, for example, has worked to ease the distress of millions of refugees who have fled their countries to escape from war and political persecution. A special unit of the Secretary-General's office has supervised and assisted free elections in more than ninety countries. It tries to establish stable and democratic governments in newly independent countries or in countries where the people have defeated a dictatorial government. Other units promote the rights of women, children, and religious and ethnic minorities. The General Assembly provides a useful setting for debate on these and other issues.

These three kinds of action—to end violence, to reduce poverty, and to promote social and political justice—all make a contribution to peace. True peace requires all three, working together.

The UN does not always succeed: like individuals, it makes mistakes . . . and it often learns from its mistakes. Despite the United Nations' occasional stumbles, over the years it has grown and moved forward. These books will show you how.

Terrorism puts the entire Earth at risk.

Chapter **1**

The United Nations and Terrorism: An Overview

*T*errorism is a global threat with global effects; . . . its consequences affect every aspect of the United Nations' agenda from development to peace to human rights and the rule of law. By its very nature, terrorism is an assault on the fundamental principles of law, order, human rights, and the peaceful settlement of disputes upon which the United Nations is established. The United Nations has an indispensable role to play in providing the legal and organizational framework within which the international campaign against terrorism can unfold.
—Kofi Annan, UN Secretary-General, October 4, 2002

Terrorists seek to create a state of fear through various means, including car bombs.

Chapter One—The United Nations and Terrorism: An Overview

From the earliest days of recorded history, humankind has perpetrated acts of terror on their fellow beings in hopes of *demoralizing* and frightening each other. Two thousand years ago, the word zealot, now used to describe anyone who is fanatical about a particular philosophy or cause, comes from the name of an ancient Jewish group that worked to expel the Romans from Judea through terrorist techniques. To send Rome a message that they were not wanted, the Zealots would attack Roman officials in broad daylight—and in front of large groups of onlookers. Many other words are now used to describe terrorists or criminals. "Assassin" (from an ancient Muslim society that attacked leaders who deviated from strict Muslim law) and "thug" (from the Thugees, a Hindu *sect* that preyed on British travelers in India) actually have their roots in terrorist actions.

Terrorism in a Modern Context

Terrorist activity affects virtually every corner of today's world. As a result, individual governments and regional and international governing bodies have been forced to address the issue.

Terrorism was first formally addressed by the League of Nations, the *predecessor* of the modern United Nations (UN). In 1937, the League of Nations drafted the Geneva Convention for the Prevention and Punishment of Terrorism. This was intended to be a vehicle by which member nations would be able to follow a consistent plan to address the underlying causes of international terrorism and to identify, try, and punish terrorists.

Despite the good intentions of the League of Nations, its plan was never widely adopted. For the next several years, individual nations *unilaterally* addressed terrorist incidents. In the decades that followed, the Convention for the Prevention and Punishment of Terrorism, the UN was formed and grew into an international body of true importance with some power to enforce its resolutions. This had never been true of the League of Nations. The League of Nations had been largely ineffective, although it was based on principles similar to the UN.

Development of Current Conventions on Terrorism

Despite the growth and increasing influence of the UN, it did not address the issue of terrorism until 1963. What emerged was a series of twelve *conventions* that dealt with international terrorism from legal and political perspectives. Instead of crafting one document to identify a single policy on terrorist activity of all types, the twelve individual conventions were drafted over a period of years as new threats were identified.

All twelve conventions have common features. Each one defines a particular type of terrorist violence as a crime under the convention. An example is hijacking an airplane. Each convention requires individual member countries to criminalize terrorist acts in its own domestic laws. Every one of the conventions also identifies certain policies by which the involved parties are required to establish *jurisdiction* over the crime, and the country where the suspect is found is obligated to establish jurisdiction over the crime in question. That country is then required to refer the crime for international prosecution if the country does not *extradite* the suspect. This requirement is commonly known as the principle of "no safe haven for terrorists." Most nations believe it is vital to deprive terrorist suspects of *havens* where they can flee and be safe from prosecution.

Although the twelve major conventions and *protocols* related to a country's responsibilities for combating terrorism would seem to provide ample protection from terrorist activity, the evening news confirm terrorist acts still occur around the world. These laws are sometimes ineffective because many countries are not yet party to these legal instruments, or they have not started to enforce them. Some believe the twelve conventions do not go far enough in identifying terrorist crimes and appropriate means of prosecution. The following list identifies the twelve major terrorism conventions and provides a brief summary of each.

Convention on Offences and Certain Other Acts Committed on Board Aircraft

This is also referred to as the Tokyo Convention of 1963, a convention that applies to terrorist acts affecting airline safety. If necessary to protect the safety of the aircraft, the law authorizes the pilot to impose reasonable measures, including restraint, on any person the pilot has reason to believe has committed or is about to commit a crime. The law also requires member states to take custody of offenders and to return control of the aircraft to the pilot or an authorized representative.

Convention for the Suppression of Unlawful Seizure of Aircraft

Also known as the Hague Convention of 1970, this law makes it a crime for any person on board an aircraft in flight to, "unlawfully, by force or threat thereof, or any other form of intimidation, [to] seize or exercise control of that aircraft" or to attempt to do so. The law requires parties to the convention to make hijackings punishable by "severe penalties." It also requires countries that have custody of offenders to either extradite the offender or submit the case for prosecution. Countries are required to assist each other in connection with criminal trials brought under the convention.

The heightened security at airports reflects the world's increased concern in response to terrorism.

The Montreal Convention defined terrorism in the skies.

Convention for the Suppression of Unlawful Acts Against the Safety of Civil Aviation

The Montreal Convention of 1971 applies to acts of aviation *sabotage*, such as bombings aboard aircraft in flight. The convention makes it a crime for any person to intentionally perform an act of violence against a person on board an aircraft in flight, if that act is likely to endanger the safety of that aircraft, to place an explosive device on an aircraft, or to attempt such acts. It is also unlawful to be an *accomplice* to a person who performs or attempts to perform such acts. The convention requires countries that are parties to the convention to make such crimes punishable by "severe penalties." Countries that have custody of offenders must either extradite the offenders or submit the case for prosecution, and countries are required to assist each other in connection with criminal trials brought under the convention.

Convention on the Prevention and Punishment of Crimes Against Internationally Protected Persons

Passed in 1973, this law outlaws attacks on senior government officials and diplomats. The convention defines internationally protected persons as a head of state, a minister for foreign affairs, or a representative or an official of a state or international organization. The law requires each country to criminalize and make punishable "by appropriate penalties which take into account their grave nature," the intentional murder, kidnapping, or other attack on an internationally protected person, a violent attack on official premises, private accommodations, or the means of transport of such a person. It is also a crime to threaten or attempt to commit such an attack or commit any act "constituting participation as an accomplice."

International Convention Against the Taking of Hostages

The Hostages Convention of 1979 is very straightforward: any person who seizes or detains and threatens to kill, to injure, or to continue to detain another person in order to compel a third party, namely, a state, an international intergovernmental organization, a natural or juridical person, or a group of persons, to do or *abstain* from doing any act as an explicit or implicit condition for the release of the hostage commits the offense of taking of hostage within the meaning of this convention. As with the other conventions, a state that is a party to the convention must criminalize hostage taking and provide for the apprehension and prosecution of hostage takers.

Convention on the Physical Protection of Nuclear Material

The Nuclear Materials Convention of 1980 combats the unlawful theft and use of nuclear material. It criminalizes the unlawful possession, use, and transfer of nuclear material; the theft of nuclear material; and threats to use nuclear material to cause death or serious injury to any person or substantial property damage.

Protocol for the Suppression of Unlawful Acts of Violence at Airports Serving International Civil Aviation, Supplementary to the Convention for the Suppression of Unlawful Acts Against the Safety of Civil Aviation

Written in 1988, this convention extends and supplements the provisions of the earlier Montreal Convention to include all terrorist acts at airports serving international civil aviation.

Convention for the Suppression of Unlawful Acts Against the Safety of Maritime Navigation

Also written in 1988, this convention applies to terrorist activities on ships and establishes a legal framework to prosecute acts against international shipping. Under this law, it is a crime for a person to seize or exercise control over a ship by force, threat, or intimidation; to perform an act of violence against a person on board a ship if that act is likely to endanger the safe navigation of the ship; or to place a destructive device or substance aboard a ship.

Protocol for the Suppression of Unlawful Acts Against the Safety of Fixed Platforms Located on the Continental Shelf

Drafted in 1988, this document applies to terrorist activities on fixed offshore platforms, like those used to drill for oil. Its legal guidelines are similar to those for terrorist acts against aircraft and ships.

The Nuclear Materials Convention sought to protect nuclear power plants from terrorist abuses.

Terrorists in Kuwait burned oil wells.

Convention on the Marking of Plastic Explosives
for the Purpose of Detection

This provision was negotiated in 1991 in response to the 1988 bombing of Pan Am Flight 103. This convention allows chemical marking to facilitate detection of plastic explosives as a means to combat aircraft sabotage. The law is designed to control and limit the use of unmarked and undetectable plastic explosives, and parties to the convention are obligated in their respective countries to ensure effective control over "unmarked" plastic explosives. Unmarked explosives are those that do not contain one of the detection agents described in the Technical Annex that accompanies the treaty. In general, each country must take specific measures to:

- prevent the manufacture of unmarked plastic explosives
- prevent the movement of unmarked plastic explosives in or out of its borders
- exercise strict control over possession and transfer of unmarked explosives made or imported prior to the date of the convention
- ensure that all stocks of such unmarked explosives not held by the military or police are destroyed within three years
- take necessary measures to ensure that unmarked plastic explosives held by the military or police are destroyed or consumed within fifteen years
- guarantee the destruction of any unmarked explosives manufactured after the date of the convention for that country.

International Convention for the Suppression of Terrorist Bombing

Created by a UN General Assembly Resolution in 1997, this convention establishes a framework for international jurisdiction over the unlawful and intentional use of explosives and other lethal devices against various defined public places with intent to kill or cause serious bodily injury, or with intent to cause extensive destruction of the public place.

International Convention for the Suppression
of the Financing of Terrorism

Drafted in 1999, this convention requires countries to take measures to prevent the direct or indirect financing of terrorists. This also applies to those groups claiming to have charitable, social, or

UN conventions seek to make the world safer for all its inhabitants.

cultural goals that engage in such ***illicit*** activities as drug trafficking or ***gunrunning***. The law requires states to hold liable those who finance terrorism for such acts; and provides for the identification, freezing, and seizure of money allocated for terrorist activities, as well as for the return of the forfeited funds to other states on a case-by-case basis.

In addition to these twelve conventions, the UN General Assembly and the Security Council have adopted several resolutions pertaining to terrorism. The laws and actions established by the UN regarding international terrorism are broad and often spread across the UN's many branches and agencies. However, the twelve formal conventions against terrorism provide a basic framework in which member nations can coordinate their antiterrorism activities.

UNITED NATIONS
PLAZA

1 AV

NO STOPPING
ANYTIME
←→
DEPT OF TRANSPORTATION

*The United Nations headquarters
is in New York City.*

Terrorism and the Security Council

T he Security Council is the most powerful branch of the UN. Its purpose is to maintain peace and security among nations. While other bodies of the UN can only make recommendations to member governments, the UN Charter gives the Security Council the power to make decisions member governments must follow. Decisions of the council are known as UN Security Council Resolutions.

Structure of the Security Council

In order for the Security Council to meet on a moment's notice, an ambassador (a country's representative) for each Security Council member must always be present at UN headquarters. This provision was implemented to address a weakness of the League of Nations—often unable to respond quickly to crises. The presidency of the Security Council rotates among members and lasts for one month. Two types of membership exist in the UN Security Council. Some nations are permanent members, while others are elected for a specified term.

The council has five permanent members: the People's Republic of China, France, the Russian Federation, the United Kingdom, and the United States of America. The permanent members were originally based on the victorious allies of World War II. Each permanent member also has the veto power to halt any resolution, a single blocking vote that outweighs any majority.

Ten other members are elected by the General Assembly for two-year terms beginning on January 1, with five replaced every year. The members are chosen by regional groups and confirmed by the UN General Assembly. The African, Latin American, and Western European *blocs* select two members each. The Arab, Asian, and Eastern European blocs select one member each. The final council seat alternates between Asian and African selections. As of September 2005, elected members are Algeria, Argentina, Benin, Brazil, Denmark, Greece, Japan, the Philippines, Romania, and Tanzania.

As the only body of the UN with the power to compel individual member states to abide by its resolutions, the Security Council has a critical role in the war against international terrorism. As a result, the Security Council has passed a number of resolutions dealing with terrorism and what individual states must do to cooperate with the UN and other governments in the prevention of terrorist activity, as well as the apprehension, extradition, and prosecution of terrorist suspects.

The Nuclear Non-Proliferation Treaty

At present, the five permanent members of the Security Council are the only nations permitted to possess nuclear weapons under the Nuclear Non-Proliferation Treaty. However, North Korea, India, Pakistan, Israel, and other countries that are not permanent members of the UN Security Council do possess nuclear weapons, despite the framework established by the UN Charter.

The Security Council in session

The terrorist attack on the Pentagon and the World Trade Center on September 11, 2001, led to Resolution 1373.

A Critical Role in the War on Terror: Resolution 1373

In recent years, the Security Council has been very active on matters regarding terrorism. This was spurred, in part, by the need to respond strongly and quickly to the terrorist attacks on New York City and Washington, D.C., as well as the airplane crash in Pennsylvania on September 11, 2001. Terrorists striking the World Trade Center not only attacked the United States but killed citizens of many different countries and caused worldwide economic damage. Charged with maintaining the world's peace and security, the Security Council felt a need to react in a way that would have a lasting and meaningful effect.

On September 28, 2001, the Security Council adopted Resolution 1373, which declared, "acts, methods and practices of terrorism are contrary to the purposes and principles of the United Nations." It required UN members to "become parties as soon as possible to the relevant international conventions and protocols" and "to increase cooperation and fully implement the relevant international conventions and protocols."

Monitoring Compliance by Member States

Resolution 1373 also established the Counter-Terrorism Committee (CTC) to monitor the implementation of the resolution and increase the capability of members to fight terrorism. The CTC has now become the UN's primary body for cooperative action against international terrorism. The committee consists of one representative from all fifteen members of the Security Council. Members of the Security Council elect the committee's chairman and vice chairmen.

Resolution 1373 imposes binding obligations on all member nations, with the aim of combating all forms of terrorism. The resolution requires that members deny all forms of financial support to terrorist groups; prevent the possibility of safe haven, *sustenance*, or support for terrorists; share information with other governments on any groups who have committed or are planning terrorist acts; cooperate with other governments in the investigation, detection, arrest, and prosecution of those involved in such acts; criminalize active and passive assistance for terrorism in domestic laws and bring violators of these laws to justice; and become party as soon as possible to the relevant international conventions and protocols relating to terrorism. The CTC demands that every member take specific actions to meet the requirements of the resolution based on the unique circumstances in each country. UN members must report to the CTC regularly to show the changes and progress their countries are making to contribute to the global war against terrorism.

UN resolutions must be carried out around the world by UN peacekeeping forces.

All reports received by the CTC are assessed by one of three subcommittees. As part of the review process, each member nation is invited to have a representative attend part of the subcommittee's discussion of the report. Independent advisers give the subcommittees technical advice. These advisers support the work of the CTC with expertise in the fields of legislative drafting, financial law and practice, customs law and practice, immigration law and practice, extradition law and practice, police and law enforcement, and illegal arms and drug trafficking. The subcommittees can also obtain additional technical assistance from advisers in other fields.

Based on the analysis of each nation's reports and other available information, the CTC assesses countries' compliance with Resolution 1373. The CTC then sends a letter to each nation, including input from any relevant experts. These letters may ask for further information on issues discussed in their reports and other matters the CTC may consider related to the implementation of the resolution. Nations are required to respond to the issues raised in the letter in another

UN delegates do the difficult work of protecting the world.

UN inspectors in Iraq sought to ensure that this nation was complying with UN regulations.

report, which is due within three months. Long-term implementation of Resolution 1373 is an ongoing process that consists of three different stages.

Stage A

In the first stage, the CTC is concerned with whether a nation has in place effective counterterrorism legislation in all areas of activity related to Resolution 1373. Specific attention is paid to financial support of terrorists. Legislation is viewed as a key issue, because without an efficient legal framework, member nations cannot develop effective means to prevent terrorism, or bring terrorists and their supporters to justice. Reviews of a country's reports will continue to focus on Stage A until the CTC has no further comments about the goals of this stage.

Stage B

This stage begins once countries have legislation in place addressing all aspects of Resolution 1373. During this phase of the resolution, a nation strengthens its governmental machinery to enforce Resolution 1373-related legislation. This includes activities designed to prevent recruitment by terrorist groups, limit the movement of terrorists, and eliminate the establishment of terrorist safe havens and any other forms of passive or active support for terrorists or terrorist groups.

To meet the requirements of effective enforcement required by Stage B, a country must have in place police and intelligence structures to detect, monitor, and apprehend those involved in and who support terrorist activities. Countries must demonstrate that customs, immigration, and border controls have been implemented to prevent the movement of terrorists and the establishment of safe havens. Finally, they must demonstrate that controls are in place preventing access to weapons by terrorists.

Stage C

The CTC recognizes that every nation is unique, and the results of these differences in circumstances mean that progress through these priorities will not be uniform. However, the CTC requires all countries show progress toward implementation of Resolution 1373 at the fastest possible speed. Stage C occurs once the CTC determines that a country has met the requirements of the previous stages. Stage C is the monitoring stage, during which the CTC makes certain that countries continue to be in ***compliance*** with the requirements.

UN Action Against Terrorism: Fighting Fear

Revitalization

Although the procedural framework established for the CTC seems to be well organized, the process of assessing the compliance of member nations has not gone as smoothly as planned. In the CTC chairman's January 26, 2004 report on the problems encountered in the implementation of the resolution, a variety of problems were identified regarding the effectiveness of the CTC. Some of these problems relate to:

- a perceived inconsistency in the evaluation of countries' efforts
- difficulties in providing adequate and acceptable technical assistance to countries that require aid in implementing the requirements of Resolution 1373
- a lack of coordination between the CTC and international, regional, and subregional organizations.

Other problems concern the support structure the CTC receives from the UN itself. These issues involve a lack of coordination between the CTC and other branches of the UN's counter-terrorism agencies. The CTC chairman also identified the lack of a defined operating budget, as well as the lack of long-term appointments for the CTC's expert advisers as serious problems.

The need for change in the CTC has become urgent as it has assumed a more active role in the UN's counterterrorism program. Security Council Resolution 1535, adopted on March 26, 2004, approved a series of methods designed to revitalize the efforts of the CTC and establish the Counter-Terrorism Committee Executive Directorate (CTED) to improve the committee's ability to monitor the implementation of Resolution 1373 and effectively continue its work. The CTED is headed by an executive director at the assistant secretary-general level.

Other Activities Against Terror

The UN Security Council has passed several other measures designed to prevent terrorism. Although the CTC remains the primary body reporting to the Security Council on the progress of individual nations in combating the spread of international terrorism, other committees assist in this important work. For example, United Nations Security Council Resolution 1540 was passed on April 28, 2004, creating the 1540 Committee.

This resolution calls on member countries to take additional measures to prevent the ***proliferation*** of nuclear, chemical, or biological weapons and their means of delivery. The 1540

Chemical weapons are as big a danger as nuclear.

*The United Nations works to ensure that all citizens of the Earth
have lives of peace and safety.*

Committee is charged with evaluating compliance in a similar manner to the way the CTC oversees general adherence with antiterrorism measures. The difference between the two bodies is that the 1540 Committee is concerned solely with measuring compliance of nations in adopting stricter methods to control the proliferation of weapons of mass destruction.

Facing a Continuing Threat

Although the Security Council has taken real and measurable steps to combat global terrorism, the struggle against this threat to the stability and prosperity of the world is far from over. This is reflected in a statement made by the president of the Security Council on September 11, 2002. The president promised the continued vigilance of the Security Council:

> The threat is real, the challenge is enormous, and the fight against terrorism will be long. The Security Council will remain steadfast against the threat that endangers all that has been achieved and all that remains to be achieved, to fulfill the principles and purposes of the United Nations for all people everywhere.

A summit-level meeting of the Security Council

Chapter

3

The United Nations and Terrorism Prevention

With a global membership and a commitment to world security, the UN is uniquely positioned to play a crucial role in the international fight against terrorism. Individual members often struggle with internal political, economic, and bureaucratic limitations. As an independent international organization, the UN has more freedom in establishing an antiterrorism agenda.

UN Action Against Terrorism: Fighting Fear

A Structure for Preventing Terrorism

The United Nations Office on Drugs and Crime (UNODC) is a critical component of the UN's efforts to prevent terrorism. Headquartered in Vienna, Austria, the UNODC has a drug program and a crime program. The crime program deals with terrorism issues through the Terrorism Prevention Branch (TPB), an agency operating under the guidance of the Division for Treaty Affairs (DTA). The TPB provides technical assistance and advisory services to countries in their fight against terrorism. As a consequence, UNODC's operational activities focus on strengthening legislation against terrorism in individual member countries.

UNODC aims at responding quickly and effectively to requests for counterterrorism assistance, in compliance with the priorities set by the Commission on Crime Prevention and Criminal Justice and the CTC. Types of assistance include reviewing domestic legislation and providing advice on drafting new laws, giving in-depth assistance on the *ratification* and implementation of new legislation against terrorism through *mentorship* programs, and offering training to national criminal justice systems on the practical application of the universal instruments against terrorism.

The United Nations works in nations around the world to help fight terrorism at the local level.

The United Nations building in Vienna

Was George Washington a freedom fighter—or a terrorist?

Terrorist—or Freedom Fighter

George Washington was a terrorist, true or false? Osama bin Ladin is a terrorist, true or false? It depends on whom you ask. After all, both used violence to attack an established government.

"One person's freedom fighter is another person's terrorist" is an often-heard statement. According to a February 2002 Harris Poll, most Americans consider acts of violence against dictatorial, military, or undemocratic governments to be the work of freedom fighters. Violence against other, nonoppressive governments are deemed acts of terrorism by the majority of Americans.

In carrying out its activities, UNODC works closely with the CTC, and an efficient working relationship has developed between the two agencies. The CTC receives and analyzes the reports received from member countries and arranges technical assistance for those in need of aid. The TPB provides this assistance. Regular contact with the CTC is maintained by sharing information and identifying with the CTC countries most in need of legislative aid. In this way, the CTC is able to direct requests for assistance from the needy countries to UNODC.

The close ties between CTC and UNODC were highlighted at the biannual special meeting of the CTC, which was attended by representatives from more than forty regional and other organizations. The Organization for Security and Co-operation in Europe (OSCE) and UNODC jointly hosted this meeting in March 2004. This resulted in the Vienna Declaration of 2004. In this declaration, representatives of the participating organizations agreed to find ways to coordinate and exchange information with the CTC and each another. They also agreed to improve cooperation and coordination by conducting joint technical assistance programs or joint visits to nations requesting aid.

Achieving Results

The benefits of this cooperation can be seen in the progress the TPB has made. Between October 2002 and June 2004, the TPB worked to educate lawmakers and criminal justice officials from over eighty countries on the provisions of Security Council Resolution 1373, and with the requirements for ratifying and implementing the universal antiterrorism instruments and international cooperation arrangements. National action plans have been developed together with individual governments as a means of setting clear and achievable goals related to terrorism prevention. Special legislative drafting committees have been established to study the provisions of the instruments and to make recommendations to governments regarding ratification, as well as the practical realization of the proposed legislation. By July 23, 2004, forty-three countries received this direct assistance, which was tailored to meet the individual needs of each nation.

Specialized workshops have been held to give countries from the same region a forum in which to compare progress, learn from each other, and harmonize legislative efforts. These workshops have produced final documents focusing on the follow-up technical assistance needs of participating countries. The TPB has supplied nations with assistance in completing reports to the CTC. Terrorism prevention experts have been strategically dispatched to a number of critical regions to support and follow up these assistance activities.

Working Partnerships

All ongoing work and all TPB activities are guided and coordinated by the CTC. When appropriate, other UN agencies are consulted. The TPB also draws on existing UNODC internal expertise, such as in the areas of *money laundering* and organized crime and corruption. In addition, the Office of Legal Affairs is also consulted on relevant matters.

Because many organizations and entities—both internal and external to the UN—are involved in the prevention and combat of terrorism, the TPB has begun to establish partnerships with relevant agencies on a number of levels. The TPB believes a global and integrated response to terrorism will help avoid duplication of efforts and resources, increase cost effectiveness, and broaden the audience each organization can reach individually.

The free exchange of expertise and information with other international, regional, and national institutions is an important tool. Some organizations regularly provide assistance to the TPB. These include the Council of Europe, the Intergovernmental Authority on Development, the International Monetary Fund, the Office of the High Commissioner for Human Rights, the Organization of American States and the Organization for Security and Cooperation in Europe. The TPB expects that partnerships with such organizations will continue to expand in order to allow an efficient response to the needs and requests of members in their terrorism prevention plans.

The United Nations provides human resources—experts and other professionals—to nations around the world, including Croatia.

The flags outside the UN building in New York City represent the nations that have committed themselves to working with the United Nations.

A Global Strategy to Prevent Terror

In addition to the various committees and bodies created by the UN to guarantee the consistent and universal application of existing resolutions dealing with terrorism, the UN secretary-general, Kofi Annan, recently unveiled a new global strategy against terrorism. On March 10, 2005, the secretary-general outlined his plan in a keynote address to the Closing Plenary of the International Summit on Democracy, Terrorism, and Security. He highlighted several areas the UN still needs to address. The main elements of this comprehensive plan can be summarized by what is now referred to as "The five Ds."

The first "D" comes from "*dissuading **disaffected** groups from choosing terrorism as a tactic.*" Groups often resort to terrorist acts because they think those tactics are effective, and often because they receive approval for their actions from religious and political leaders. A frequently quoted phrase in some parts of the world states, "One man's terrorist is another man's freedom fighter." Kofi Annan's plan includes applying pressure to ensure all political and moral authorities proclaim terrorism unacceptable. It is also *imperative* that terrorist acts committed to achieve a specific goal—for example, to obtain the release of a prisoner—prove ineffective.

Finally, in accomplishing the first "D," Kofi Annan proposed a measure that many in the international community have been seeking for some time. Citing a report issued by a High-Level Panel on Terrorism, the secretary-general stated:

> The Panel calls for a definition of terrorism which would make it clear that any action constitutes terrorism if it is intended to cause death or serious bodily harm to civilians and non-combatants, with the purpose of intimidating a population or compelling a Government or an international organization to do or abstain from any act. I believe this proposal has clear

UN peacekeepers on patrol

The fifth of the UN's Ds—defend human rights—seeks to protect all human beings on our planet.

moral force, and I strongly urge world leaders to unite behind it. Not only political leaders, but civil society and religious leaders should clearly denounce terrorist tactics as criminal and inexcusable.

This is a significant development as the UN has debated an official definition of terrorism for years without reaching a consensus.

The second "D" comes from "*denying* terrorists the means to carry out their attacks."

Chapter Three—The United Nations and Terrorism Prevention

Although the UN already has many measures in place to prevent the financing of terrorist activities, gaps remain. Provisions outlined in this new strategy include taking effective action against money laundering. One way the UN could act on this matter would be to adopt the eight Special Recommendations on Terrorist Financing produced by the OECD's Financial Action Task Force.

In addition to denying terrorists funding, it is critical to not give them access to nuclear materials. In his remarks, the secretary-general established the link between a nuclear attack and the economic crisis that would inevitably follow. With a major economic crisis, poverty increases and affects things like infant mortality. In other words, regardless of what country sustains the attack, the effects of the attack would be felt around the globe. As a result, the secretary-general urged the UN member countries to universally adopt, without delay, the international convention on nuclear terrorism.

The third "D" represents "*deter* states from supporting terrorist groups." This is easily accomplished by strengthening **sanctions** and other **coercive** measures available to the Security Council to encourage nations to stop harboring terrorist groups.

The fourth "D" stands for "*develop* state capacity to prevent terrorism." As described earlier, the UN has performed a great deal of work in this regard. The CTC and the TPB are working to develop domestic systems in poor nations to protect them from **exploitation** by terrorist groups. However, the secretary-general identified additional ways the international community can assist the world's poorest nations in resisting terrorist groups and their influence.

The United Nations Development Program and its Electoral Assistance Division have critical roles in assisting with the establishment of stable forms of government. Legitimate and fair elections can be monitored by these bodies, and they have many resources at their disposal to help strengthen young democratic states.

Terrorists with **extremist** philosophies often target uneducated people holding narrow worldviews. Therefore, it is necessary the international community promotes the availability of education and a free press in disadvantaged areas of the world. The United Nations Education, Scientific and Cultural Organization (UNESCO) can play a vital role in promoting education and reducing the vulnerability of the general population to distorted ideology in the developing world.

In developing the world's capacity to prevent terrorism, one critical area has been ignored even by many industrialized nations. A comprehensive defense system against **bioterrorism** has yet to be established. The secretary-general has called for a major initiative to create such systems.

The fifth "D" is for "*defend* human rights." The secretary-general voiced concern that some policies implemented to combat terror have infringed on individual rights. As a potential solution, he called for the creation of a special representative to report to the Commission on Human Rights on the compatibility of counterterrorism measures with international human rights laws.

Kofi Annan

Chapter Three—The United Nations and Terrorism Prevention

Secretary-General Annan also established a special implementation task force to monitor the progress in implementing his new strategy and to coordinate the efforts of all UN agencies involved in this endeavor.

Looking Toward the Future

The UN has taken action to prevent terror on many fronts. The accomplishments of the CTC and the TPB have been effective and measurable. New legislation and security measures implemented as a result of these efforts have made it more difficult for terrorist groups to operate in many areas of the world. New strategies outlined by the secretary-general give a clear and organized course of action as the global community continues its important work preventing acts of terror.

The September 11 attacks made Americans much more aware of terrorists.

Chapter 4

The United Nations and al Qaeda

The attacks of September 11, 2001, increased public awareness of the al Qaeda terrorist network. However, international justice officials and individual governments had been aware of the threat presented by al Qaeda for years before the devastating attacks. The UN had also dealt with issues pertaining to the terrorist network prior to September 11. To understand current policies pertaining to al Qaeda, one must first understand that organization's long and bloody history.

A History of al Qaeda

Al Qaeda is Arabic for "the base," and the organization was founded by a wealthy Saudi business-man named Osama bin Laden in the early 1980s. His initial goal was to support the war in Afghanistan, where Afghan Muslims were fighting to free their country from Soviet occupation. The Muslim victory in Afghanistan fueled the *jihad* movement. Trained fighters called *muja-hedin*, who had gone to Afghanistan to fight against the Soviets, began returning to countries including Egypt, Algeria, and Saudi Arabia. They brought back extensive experience in *guerrilla* warfare and a desire to continue the jihad.

Sometime in 1989, al Qaeda dedicated itself to opposing non-Islamic governments through force and violence. Al Qaeda began to provide training camps and guesthouses in various coun-tries for the use of the organization and its affiliated groups. With their extreme interpretation of Islam, they recruited young men from all over the world. The organization sought to recruit U.S. citizens who could travel easily throughout the Western world to deliver messages and perform financial transactions for the benefit of al Qaeda and its affiliated groups—and to help carry out operations. By 1990, al Qaeda was providing military and intelligence training for itself and its partners. This training occurred in Afghanistan, Pakistan, and the Sudan.

Al Qaeda's initial objective was to drive U.S. armed forces out of Saudi Arabia and Somalia by any means necessary. Members of al Qaeda issued *fatwahs*, special statements on Islamic law, indicating such attacks were righteous and necessary. Al Qaeda regards its enemies in the West,

Jihad

When asked to define "jihad," many Americans might say it refers to a violent holy war waged by Muslims against non-Muslims. Although that is one definition, it is not the only one.

A "jihad" is a crusade for principles or a belief. In the context of Islam, it refers to the defense and spread of Islam and does allow violence for that purpose if it is deemed necessary. But there are also nonviolent ways to defend Islam, such as getting a reli-gious education and writing and speaking to promote Islam.

There is a third type of jihad, the "inner jihad," also called the "Greater Jihad." This jihad refers to each Muslim's internal struggle for "spiritual self-control."

The terrorist group known as al Qaeda seldom uses that name to refer to itself. According to Osama bin Laden, they used to call their camp "al Qaeda," meaning the base, and the name stuck. Others claim the United States government began using the name based on a file found on bin Laden's computer.

Al Qaeda was active in countries like Egypt.

Which Is Correct: Osama or Usama?

Actually, both are proper. Osama is the spelling used by most English-language media. U.S. secretary of defense Donald Rumsfeld, the FBI, and some media outlets prefer Usama. Less common variations are Ussamah and Oussama.

including the United States, as *infidel* nations that provide essential support for other infidel nations. The presence of U.S. armed forces in the Gulf, along with the arrest, conviction, and imprisonment in the United States of al Qaeda members, prompted fatwahs supporting attacks against U.S. interests, domestic and foreign, civilian and military. Those fatwahs resulted in attacks against the United States in locations around the world, including Somalia, Kenya, Tanzania, Yemen, Spain, Great Britain, and the United States. Both the 1993 and 2001 attacks on the World Trade Center in New York City have been attributed to al Qaeda. Since 1993, thousands of people have died in al Qaeda-provoked attacks around the world.

Over the years, al Qaeda has been headquartered in Sudan, Pakistan, and Afghanistan. Several businesses, both legal and illegal, provided income and cover to al Qaeda operatives. In the years before the attacks of September 11, 2001, al Qaeda was believed to be headquartered in the rural areas of Afghanistan, where the members were given safe haven by the radical Taliban government. The Taliban ruled Afghanistan as a Muslim *theocracy*, and all law in the country was based on a very strict and narrow interpretation of Islam.

UN Action Against al Qaeda

In the wake of a number of terrorist attacks by al Qaeda and its affiliated groups, the UN first dealt specifically with al Qaeda in Security Council Resolution 1267, which was adopted on October 15, 1999. In that document, the Security Council cited concerns about human rights violations in Afghanistan and various other violations of international law by the Taliban government. The document also addressed the obligations of the Taliban government to assist in the extradition and prosecution of al Qaeda members.

The resolution lists a series of failures by the Taliban government to meet its obligations under international law. Many of these related directly to Taliban support of the al Qaeda network. Some of the violations outlined by the Security Council include:

In the years before September 11, 2001, al Qaeda was believed to be headquartered in rural Afghanistan.

On patrol in Afghanistan

1. "the continuing use of Afghan territory, especially areas controlled by the Taliban, for the sheltering and training of terrorists and planning of terrorist acts."
2. "the fact that the Taliban continues to provide safe haven to Usama bin Laden and to allow him and others associated with him to operate a network of terrorist training camps from Taliban-controlled territory and to use Afghanistan as a base from which to sponsor international terrorist operations, noting the indictment of Usama bin Laden and his associates by the United States of America for, . . . the 7 August 1998 bombings of the United States embassies in Nairobi, Kenya, and Dar es Salaam, Tanzania and for conspiring to kill American nationals outside the United States, and noting also the request of the United States of America to the Taliban to surrender them for trial."

A mine marker in Afghanistan

The religion of Islam should not be blamed for al Qaeda's terrorist activities.

The resolution declared that these failures by the Taliban government to comply with international law constituted a threat to international peace and security, and lists a series of demands and sanctions the Security Council will impose if the Taliban does not comply. The resolution lists these in plain language. Among the main provisions made by the Security Council were:

1. "That the Afghan faction known as the Taliban, which also calls itself the Islamic Emirate of Afghanistan, comply promptly with its previous resolutions and in particular cease the provision of sanctuary and training for international terrorists and their organizations, take appropriate effective measures to ensure that the territory under its control is not used for terrorist installations and camps, or for the preparation or organization of terrorist acts against other States or their citizens, and cooperate with efforts to bring indicted terrorists to justice.

2. "That the Taliban turn over Usama bin Laden without further delay to appropriate authorities in a country where he has been indicted, or to appropriate authorities in a country where he will be returned to such a country, or to appropriate authorities in a country where he will be arrested and effectively brought to justice.

3. "That on 14 November 1999 all States shall impose the measures set out in paragraph 4 below, unless the Council has previously decided, on the basis of a report of the Secretary-General, that the Taliban has fully complied with the obligation set out in paragraph 2 above.

4. "Decides further that, in order to enforce paragraph 2 above, all States shall:
(a) "Deny permission for any aircraft to take off from or land in their territory if it is owned, leased or operated by or on behalf of the Taliban as designated by the Committee established by paragraph 6 below, unless the particular flight has been approved in advance by the Committee on the grounds of humanitarian need, including religious obligation such as the performance of the *Hajj*;

(b) "Freeze funds and other financial resources, including funds derived or generated from property owned or controlled directly or indirectly by the Taliban, or by any undertaking owned or controlled by the Taliban, . . . and ensure that neither they nor any other funds or financial resources so designated are made available, by their nationals or by any persons within their territory, to or for the benefit of the Taliban or any undertaking owned or controlled, directly or indirectly, by the Taliban, except as may be authorized by the Committee on a case-by-case basis on the grounds of humanitarian need.

Afghanistan's flag

5. "Urges all States to cooperate with efforts to fulfill the demand in paragraph 2 above, and to consider further measures against Usama bin Laden and his associates."

Although the Security Council made clear demands of the Taliban and outlined specific methods to be used to force the Taliban's compliance, the Security Council was unsuccessful in persuading the Taliban government to change its policies on any issues addressed by Resolution 1267. In 2000, the Security Council passed another resolution, further increasing the sanctions imposed on Afghanistan and freezing the personal assets of Osama bin Laden and his known al Qaeda associates. These sanctions had little effect. Afghanistan continued to provide a safe base from which al Qaeda could carry out its terrorist activities.

No Safe Haven

Following the attacks of September 11, 2001, it was soon obvious to international authorities that al Qaeda was responsible. The UN responded with a series of resolutions designed specifically to target al Qaeda and curtail their activities worldwide. Eliminating nations where the terrorists could find a safe haven became the international community's top priority. On this basis the United States, together with other nations, eventually took military action against the Taliban government. The UN responded to the attacks with a series of measures designed to increase its power in dealing with all kinds of terrorism. Through a series of resolutions, the Security Council drafted a strategy to fight al Qaeda and to monitor the progress of member nations in implementing this strategy.

The Security Council established the 1267 Committee to monitor the implementation by member nations of the sanctions it imposed on individuals and entities related to the Taliban, Osama bin Laden, or al Qaeda. The committee maintains a list of individuals and entities for this purpose. In the resolutions that followed 1267, the Security Council required all member countries to freeze assets of every person and entity on the list. Also, member countries are obligated to prevent anyone on the list from entering or traveling through their countries, and to prevent the direct or indirect supply, sale, or transfer of arms and military equipment to anyone on the list.

The fight to prevent the growth of the al Qaeda network and to bring those who have been involved with its terrorist acts to justice is the ongoing work of the Security Council and the 1267 Committee. On December 1, 2004, Heraldo Muñoz of Chile, the chairman of the 1267 Committee, addressed the Security Council. He stated, "The threat posed by Al Qaeda and the Taliban must remain the top international concern."

Chinook military helicopters flying over Afghanistan

Military, law enforcement, and legislative actions have severely restricted the global activities of al Qaeda. The network has reorganized itself, exchanging the centralized structure of the past for a global network of loosely affiliated cells whose main identifying feature is a common and extreme ideology. What has emerged is a threat that is just as real, but more difficult to confront and track. UN experts agree work remains to be done before al Qaeda no longer interferes with the world's international peace and prosperity.

The threat of terrorism endangers the world's freedom in more ways than one.

Chapter 5

The United Nations and Terrorism's Aftermath

In addition to the many policies the UN has developed to prevent terrorism, it also has a ***mandate*** to assist those devastated by the effects of terror. As the world's leading international body, the UN has a unique ability to respond to crises worldwide. The type of assistance available is based on the type of attack and the ability of the affected population to cope with the aftermath of an attack.

When scientists discovered how to split the atom to create nuclear energy, they also unleashed one of the world's most terrifying weapons.

Emergency Humanitarian Aid

Terrorist attacks have far-reaching effects. In addition to loss of life or destruction of property, often the economy is damaged. When the population suffering the attack is in an underdeveloped area of the world, economic devastation can make it impossible to obtain even the most basic necessities. When a country's food supply is endangered, the UN *subsidiary* World Food Programme (WFP) is often the first line of defense. The WFP is the world's largest humanitarian organization.

Hunger is a consequence of many types of emergencies, including natural disasters like the tsunami tragedy in Asia, to manmade crises such as civil war or major terrorist attacks. Increased civil conflict, war, and natural disasters in the world's poorest nations have caused an explosion in food emergencies. Whatever the cause of an emergency, the WFP is the primary tool of the UN's humanitarian response.

As the threat of large-scale, catastrophic terrorism looms, the WFP has established a new protocol for emergency response that can be applied to a variety of food emergencies. The first step is to conduct an emergency needs assessment to establish whether international food and non-food assistance is warranted. Often an emergency needs assessment is conducted in conjunction with other UN agencies. This approach to providing aid immediately following a disaster helps ensure that assistance programs are swiftly implemented in the event a terrorist attack disrupts the food or water supply.

Responding to a Nuclear or Radiological Attack

In matters relating to atomic energy, the UN relies on its affiliation with the International Atomic Energy Agency (IAEA). In 1986, a twenty-four-hour operational headquarters, the Emergency Response Centre (ERC), was established in Vienna, Austria. The ERC is a central body to which nations and international organizations can promptly and effectively direct initial warnings, advisory messages, requests for emergency assistance, and information.

As the threat of nuclear terrorism has grown over the last few decades, it has become clear that timely and appropriate action in the aftermath of such an attack will be necessary to save as many lives as possible, as well as address the political and social effects of such an act. In September 2003, the IAEA passed a resolution to develop a plan of action for strengthening the international emergency response for a nuclear accident or terrorist attack. Its board of governors approved the plan in June 2004. The international action plan covers three main areas: interna-

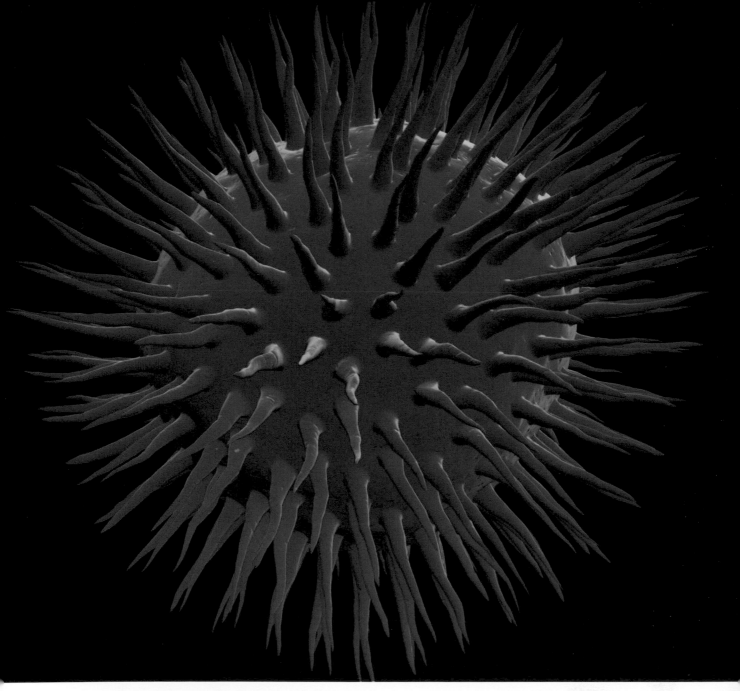

Under the right circumstances, a tiny virus can be a more deadly weapon than any gun or bomb.

tional communication, international assistance, and creation of a sustainable *infrastructure* of preparedness and response to a nuclear or radiological emergency.

The IAEA also works directly with other international bodies to provide a coordinated international response on as many fronts as possible. The Food and Agriculture Organization of the United Nations (FAO), the World Meteorological Organization (WMO), and the World Health Organization (WHO) are full parties and important partners to the Convention on Early Notification of a Nuclear Accident (CENNA) and the Convention on Assistance in the Case of a Nuclear Accident or Radiological Emergency (CANARE). Individual governments also have their own response programs in place, and the IAEA and these other UN-affiliated groups are working to enhance rather than replace those systems.

Responding to a Biological or Chemical Attack

In today's world of rapidly evolving technology, some scientific advances prove to hold as much threat as benefit. This is especially true when considering the availability of biological and chemical agents to terrorists. Several small attacks of this nature have already occurred as forms of domestic terrorism.

In March 1995, members of a Japanese religious sect named the Aum Shinrikyo (Supreme Truth) placed opened containers of a liquefied form of *sarin* on five different cars on the Tokyo subway system. Twelve people were killed in that chemical attack; five thousand required medical

Aum Shinrikyo

The Japanese cult Aum Shinrikyo was virtually unknown in the West until the sarin attack on the Tokyo subway. Founded in 1986 by Asahara Shoko, the group was heavily focused on the end of the world.

The attack on the subway system, as well as other violent acts, led to the indictment of Asahara. In 2000, under a new leader, the group changed its name to Aleph, "beginning," and started on a campaign to change its image.

attention. Anthrax attacks occurred in the United States in 2001, killing five people. The deadly bacteria was grown in a very low-tech environment and transported through the U.S. mail. Although these attacks have been small and domestic in nature, the international community cannot discount the possibility of a large-scale international attack of this type.

The UN has a significant role to play following a biological or chemical attack. Which UN organizations are involved depends on the circumstances of the attack and the population affected. They may include the UN Security Council. As the use or threat of use of chemical or biological weapons clearly constitutes a threat to international peace and security, it will therefore fall within the responsibility of the Security Council to investigate such attacks.

If it is a large-scale attack, the UN can provide humanitarian assistance. The Emergency Relief Coordinator of the United Nations was mandated by the General Assembly in 1992 to serve as the focal point and coordinating official for UN emergency relief operations. The coordinator is also the under secretary-general for Humanitarian Affairs and is supported by the UN Office for the Coordination of Humanitarian Affairs (OCHA).

OCHA

The OCHA has established an emergency response system for coordinating actions taken by the international community to deal with natural disasters and environmental emergencies, including terrorist acts. It is responsible for mobilizing and organizing international disaster response and can be contacted on a twenty-four-hour basis in case of a crisis. In humanitarian emergencies, OCHA can:

- administer requests for assistance from member nations;
- organize, in conjunction with the affected country, a needs assessment
- serve as the central coordinating agency between governments, intergovernmental organizations, nongovernmental organizations, and the UN
- provide combined information on all humanitarian emergencies
- promote, in close collaboration with other concerned organizations, the smooth transition from aid to rehabilitation.

The OCHA's Military and Civil Defense Unit (MCDU) is the core of the UN humanitarian system for the mobilization and coordination of military and civil defense assistance if needed in response to humanitarian emergencies.

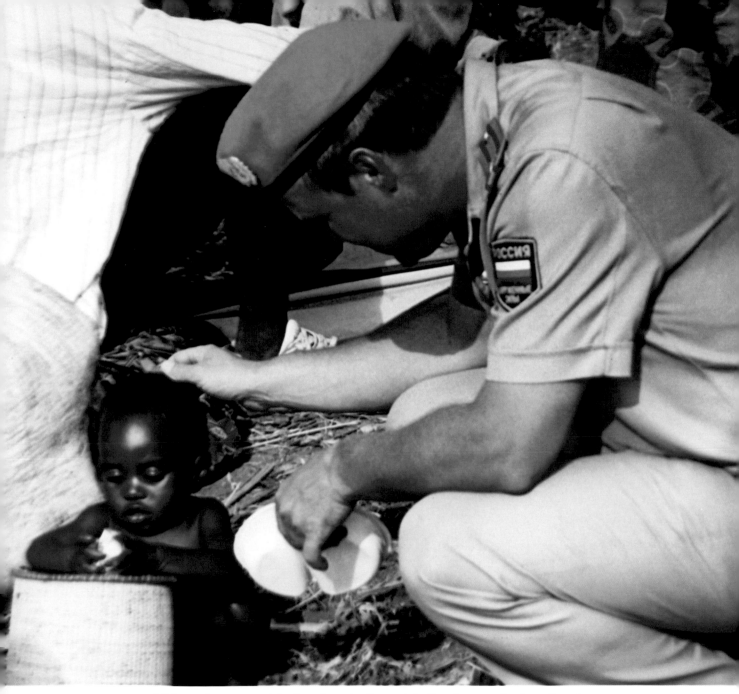

UN workers provide food and other aid after humanitarian disasters.

The OPCW provides medical teams to member nations after a chemical crisis.

WFP

As mentioned previously, the WFP can provide emergency food and associated assistance in response to humanitarian disasters arising from the use of biological or chemical weapons. These include situations in which crops or food supplies are destroyed or made unsafe, large-scale environmental damage affects people's employment, outbreaks of **_debilitating_** diseases threaten longer-term food security, or populations are displaced.

OPCW

The Organization for the Prohibition of Chemical Weapons (OPCW) is another UN body specifically created to deal with issues regarding the use of chemical weapons. The assistance available from the OPCW following a chemical attack falls into two categories: hardware (mainly protective equipment) and a variety of assistance teams.

Hardware consists largely of personal protective equipment, primarily for use by civilians. Unfortunately, at best the delivery of such equipment to an affected area will take several days. The use of personal protective equipment also requires training. This training is currently available from the OPCW on request. Other assistance-related training courses are also arranged by the OPCW, together with various member nations. These include courses for medical personnel, courses in the use of analytical equipment, and courses on the conduct of emergency assistance and rescue operations. Assistance provided by the OPCW to member countries may include medical teams, detection teams, decontamination teams, and teams for providing the necessary infrastructure support for assistance operations.

WHO

The WHO is a specialized agency of the UN. It has 192 member nations, and its secretariat includes headquarters in Geneva, six regional offices, and 141 separate country offices. According to its constitution, the purpose of the organization is to:

- act as a coordinating agency on all international health issues.
- furnish technical assistance and emergency aid upon the request or acceptance of governments.
- provide information, advice and assistance in the field of health.

The United Nations is working hard to protect the world from terrorism.

The World Organization on Animal Health is concerned with researching and preventing the spread of avian flu.

- develop, institute, and support international standards with regard to food safety and biological, pharmaceutical, and similar products.

The use of chemical or biological weapons on a large scale would likely result in catastrophic public health and medical emergencies, including a sudden and significant increase in the numbers of illnesses and deaths from a variety of diseases. In view of its mandate, the WHO would play a critical role in responding to any such emergency.

The Role of Other UN Bodies

The FAO and the World Organization on Animal Health may also have important roles to play following a biological or chemical attack. Although neither body currently has a specific terror-oriented committee, both organizations are prepared to respond to any emergency affecting crops or livestock, as a chemical or biological attack would likely do.

The FAO is prepared to respond to a biological or chemical attack within its broad mandate to provide technical and humanitarian assistance. In recent years, the FAO has contributed significantly in emergency relief and rehabilitation when droughts, floods, earthquakes, war, civil strife, and natural and manmade disasters have compromised crops and food supplies.

At first, the World Organization on Animal Health may not appear to have relevance to terrorism or its effects, but the ongoing sharing of information on the occurrence, prevention, and control of animal diseases is relevant to this objective. For example, anthrax occurs as a mild disease in cattle but can be fatal to humans. The World Organization on Animal Health has established an information system to collect and ***disseminate*** information on outbreaks of animal diseases most serious to animal and public health.

Work in Progress

The UN has many programs in place to cope effectively with what remains after a terrorist attack. However, most of the UN's subsidiary bodies still have plans in progress to upgrade their abilities to respond should disaster strike. The General Assembly and the Security Council work daily on strategies dealing with terrorism-related issues. As those efforts begin to bear fruit, the world's preeminent international body will have a greater ability to prevent terrorism and address its aftereffects.

Time Line

1937	The League of Nations drafts the Geneva Convention for the Prevention and Punishment of Terrorism.
1963	The UN passes the Convention on Offenses and Certain Other Acts Committed On Board Aircraft.
1970	The UN passes the Convention for the Suppression of Unlawful Seizure of Aircraft.
1971	The UN passes the Convention for the Suppression of Unlawful Acts Against the Safety of Civil Aviation.
1973	The UN passes the Convention on the Prevention and Punishment of Crimes Against Internationally Protected Persons.
1979	The UN passes the International Convention Against the Taking of Hostages and the Convention on the Physical Protection of Nuclear Material.
1986	The Emergency Response Centre (ERC) is established in Vienna, Austria.
1988	The UN passes the Protocol for the Suppression of Unlawful Acts of Violence at Airports Serving International Civil Aviation, supplementary to the Convention for the Suppression of Unlawful Acts Against the Safety of Civil Aviation, and the Convention for the Suppression of Unlawful Acts Against the Safety of Maritime Navigation and the Protocol for the Suppression of Unlawful Acts Against the Safety of Fixed Platforms Located on the Continental Shelf.
1991	The UN passes the Convention on the Marking of Plastic Explosives for the Purpose of Detection; the UN General Assembly mandates the Emergency Relief Coordinator of the United Nations to oversee emergency humanitarian aid.
1997	The UN passes the International Convention for the Suppression of Terrorist Bombing and the International Convention for the Suppression of the Financing of Terrorism. The Security Council adopts resolution 1267, defining the obligations of the Taliban government to assist in the extradition and prosecution of al Qaeda members.
2000	Sanctions against the Taliban are increased as the Afghan government fails to meet the demands of Resolution 1267.
2001	Al Qaeda terrorists attack the United States, and the Security Council adopts Resolution 1373, creating the CTC. The IAEA passes a resolution to develop a plan of action for strengthening the international emergency response for a nuclear accident or terrorist attack.
2004	The Security Council passes Resolution 1535, designed to revitalize the efforts of the CTC and establishes the Counter-Terrorism Committee Executive Directorate. The Security Council passes Resolution 1540.
2006	The UN continues to fight terrorism around the world.

Glossary

abstain: To not do something.

accomplice: Someone associated with another person, usually in wrongdoing.

adherence: Sticking to a belief or practice.

bioterrorism: Acts of violence involving biological weapons intended to achieve specific goals through the use of fear.

blocs: United groups of countries or organizations.

coercive: Intending to dominate by force.

compliance: Conforming to a regulation or law.

conventions: Agreements between countries, less formal than treaties.

debilitating: Reducing strength or energy.

demoralizing: Discouraging, creating a loss of confidence.

disaffected: Discontented toward authority.

disseminate: To spread.

exploitation: Unfair treatment or use of somebody or something.

extradite: To return someone accused of a crime by a different legal authority to that authority for trial or punishment.

extremist: Having to do with radical political or religious beliefs.

guerrilla: Having to do with unorganized and independent warfare carried out by independent units through harassment and sabotage.

gunrunning: Trafficking in guns and ammunition.

Hajj: The pilgrimage to Mecca that is a religious obligation of adult Muslims.

havens: Places of safety.

illicit: Illegal.

imperative: Absolutely necessary.

infidel: Someone who has no belief in the religion of the speaker or writer.

infrastructure: A region or state's basic organizational structure, made up of roads, buildings, and other public resources.

jihad: A campaign by Muslims in defense of the Islamic faith.

jurisdiction: The area over which legal authority extends.

mandate: An official instruction by an authority.

mentorship: The act of serving as a guide or tutor.

money laundering: The transferring of illegally obtained money through various businesses and accounts to make it appear the money came from a legitimate source.

predecessor: Something or someone who came before.

proliferation: The rapid spread of something.

protocols: Preliminary memoranda often formulated and signed by diplomatic negotiators as the bases for final conventions or treaties.

ratification: The act of formally approving something.

sabotage: Destructive action against a government.

sanctions: Penalties for breaking laws or agreements.

sarin: An extremely toxic gas that attacks the central nervous system, causing convulsions and death.

sect: A religious group with beliefs and practices different from those of a more established main group.

subsidiary: A group controlled by a larger one.

sustenance: Something, especially food, that supports life.

theocracy: A government governed by God or his priests.

unilaterally: Done with input from only one side of a matter.

Further Reading

Lowry, Mike. *What's Next for the UN? Understanding Global Issues.* Mankato, Minn.: Smart Apple Media, 2003.

Nye, Joseph S., Paul Wilkinson, and Yukio Satoh. *Addressing the New International Terrorism: Prevention, Intervention, and Multilateral Cooperation.* Washington, D.C.: Brookings Institution Press, 2003.

Osman, Mohamed Awad. *The United Nations and Peace Enforcement: Wars, Terrorism and Democracy.* Hampshire, UK: Ashgate Publishing, 2002.

Riggs, Robert E., Jack C. Plano, and Lawrence Ziring. *United Nations: International Organization and World Politics.* Belmont, Calif.: Wadsworth Publishing, 1999.

Weiss, Thomas G. *Terrorism and the UN: Before and after September 11.* Indianapolis: Indiana University Press, 2004.

For More Information

Food and Agriculture Organization of the United Nations
www.fao.org

Organization for the Prohibition of Chemical Weapons
www.opcw.org

UN Counter-Terrorism Committee
www.un.org/Docs/sc/committees/1373

United Nations Office for the Coordination of Humanitarian Affairs
www.reliefweb.int/ocha_ol/index.html

World Food Program
www.wfp.org

World Health Organization
www.who.int

World Organization for Animal Health (OIE)
www.oie.int

Publisher's note:
The Web sites listed on this page were active at the time of publication. The publisher is not responsible for Web sites that have changed their addresses or discontinued operation since the date of publication. The publisher will review and update the Web-site list upon each reprint.

Reports and Projects

Maps
• Use a map of the world to indicate the locations of terrorist attacks that have occurred over the last ten years.

Reports
• Write a brief report on one of the twelve international conventions against terrorism and why it was adopted.
• Research a natural or man-made disaster and how the UN responded to the crisis. What type of assistance was provided? How was this disaster similar to a terrorist attack? Do you think the same kind of emergency response would be effective in the case of a terrorist attack?
• Write a report on one of the UN's subsidiary bodies and its role in combating global terrorism.

Biographies
Write a one-page biography on one of the following:
• Kofi Annan
• Osama bin Laden

Group Activities
• One criticism of the UN is that they have yet to agree on a universal definition of terrorism. Have each member of the group choose a country to represent and meet to draft a definition of terrorism. How does the view of a representative from China differ from the definition favored by France or Iran?
• Create a fictional terrorist attack. Identify the location of the attack, the perpetrator, and the method of attack. Have each student in the group represent a current member of the Security Council. Draft a resolution responding to this terrorist attack. Identify any new steps to prevent similar attacks in the future. Explain how to implement new plans and measure cooperation of other nations.

Bibliography

American Society of International Law. http://www.asil.org.

Encyclopedia of Psychology. http://www.psychology.org/links/People_and_History.

Global Terrorism and the United Nations. http://www.un-globalsecurity.org.

Swiss Division of Economics and Financial Affairs.
    http://www.eda.admin.ch/sub_ecfin/e/home/docus/terror.html.

Terrorism files. http://www.terrorismfiles.org/organisations/al_qaida.html.

"The UN Acts Against Terrorism." http://www.un.org/terrorism.

United Nations Counter-Terrorism Committee. http://www.un.org/Docs/sc/committees/1373.

U.S. Department of State. http://www.state.gov.

Index

Picture Credits

Corel: pp. 18, 20, 25, 28, 29, 30, 36, 38, 43, 45, 71, 74
iStock: pp. 13, 22, 56, 57, 68
       PJ Cutsinger p. 10
       Stefan Klein p. 33
       Andreas Steinbach p. 39
       Camilo Jimenez p. 44
       Luke Daniek p. 53
       Berthold Englemann p. 55
       Eli Mordechai p. 58
       Krista Weber p. 60
       Yakov Munkebo p. 62
       Carmen Martinez Banús p. 64
       George Argyropoulos p. 66
Photos.com: pp. 8, 14, 17, 34, 46, 72
United Nations: p. 48
www.freepictures.com: p. 50

To the best knowledge of the publisher, all other images are in the public domain. If any image has been inadvertently uncredited, please notify Harding House Publishing Service, Vestal, New York 13850, so that rectification can be made for future printings.

Biographies

Author

Heather Docalavich first became interested in the work of the United Nations while working as an adviser for a high school Model UN program. She lives in Hilton Head Island, South Carolina, with her four children.

Series Consultant

Bruce Russett is Dean Acheson Professor of Political Science at Yale University and editor of the *Journal of Conflict Resolution*. He has taught or researched at Columbia, Harvard, M.I.T., Michigan, and North Carolina in the United States, and educational institutions in Belgium, Britain, Israel, Japan, and the Netherlands. He has been president of the International Studies Association and the Peace Science Society, holds an honorary doctorate from Uppsala University in Sweden. He was principal adviser to the U.S. Catholic Bishops for their pastoral letter on nuclear deterrence in 1985, and co-directed the staff for the 1995 Ford Foundation Report, *The United Nations in Its Second Half Century.* He has served as editor of the *Journal of Conflict Resolution* since 1973. The twenty-five books he has published include *The Once and Future Security Council* (1997), *Triangulating Peace: Democracy, Interdependence, and International Organizations* (2001), *World Politics: The Menu for Choice* (8th edition 2006), and *Purpose and Policy in the Global Community* (2006).